Disney's Aladdin

Illustrated by Phil Ortiz and Serge Michaels

A Random House PICTUREBACK® Book
Random House 🏠 New York

Copyright © 2004 Disney Enterprises, Inc. All rights reserved under International and Pan-American Copyright Conventions. Published in the United States by Random House Children's Books, a division of Random House, Inc., New York, and simultaneously in Canada by Random House of Canada Limited, Toronto, in conjunction with Disney Enterprises, Inc. PICTUREBACK, RANDOM HOUSE, and the Random House colophon are registered trademarks of Random House, Inc. Originally published in slightly different form by Golden Books in 1992.

Library of Congress Control Number: 2003110084   ISBN: 0-7364-2033-9

www.randomhouse.com/kids/disney   Printed in the United States of America   10 9 8 7 6 5 4 3 2 1

One night, two horsemen raced across the Arabian desert, chasing a winged medallion. When it stopped, the men watched as the sand rose up to form a huge tiger's head with an open mouth.

"At last—the Cave of Wonders!" marveled Jafar, the Sultan's chief adviser. "Remember, bring me the lamp," he said to Gazeem. "Then the rest of the treasure is yours."

As Gazeem stepped into the cave, a ghostly voice boomed, "Only one may enter here! The diamond in the rough." Suddenly, the cave's entrance clamped shut, trapping Gazeem inside. The tiger's head quickly dissolved into the sand.

"We must get that lamp!" Jafar said to Iago, his wicked parrot. "Obviously, Gazeem was less than worthy. We must find the diamond in the rough."

The next day, in the nearby city of Agrabah, a poor young peasant named Aladdin and his monkey, Abu, were being chased through the marketplace. They had taken a loaf of bread. Aladdin and Abu managed to slip away from the palace guards and find safety behind a high wall.

Aladdin and Abu could hardly wait to eat. But when Aladdin saw two hungry children staring up at him, he gave the bread to them.

That night Aladdin and Abu returned to their rooftop home. "Someday, Abu, things are going to change," said Aladdin. "We'll be rich and live in a palace!"

Meanwhile, at the Sultan's palace, Princess Jasmine was not happy. According to the law, she had to marry a prince by her birthday, which was only three days away.

"Father, I don't like being forced into this," Jasmine confessed. "If I do marry, I want it to be for love."

Jasmine was so sad that she decided to run away, even though she had never been outside the palace grounds. Soon she found herself in the marketplace—and in trouble.

She took an apple from a cart and gave it to a hungry child.

"You'd better be able to pay for that!" said the fruit seller.

"I don't have any money!" cried Jasmine.

Suddenly, Aladdin dashed up and claimed to be her brother. "She's a little crazy," he told the fruit seller.

Aladdin and Jasmine went racing through the marketplace.
But a guard seized Aladdin. "Unhand him!" Jasmine cried.

"Princess Jasmine!" said the guard, surprised. "I would, but
my orders come from Jafar."

Jasmine hurried back to the palace to find Jafar.

Jasmine found Jafar in his chambers and demanded that Aladdin be released.

"Sadly, the boy's sentence has already been carried out—death," answered Jafar.

"How could you?" cried Jasmine, heartbroken.

Jasmine did not know it, but Jafar was lying. He had discovered that Aladdin was the diamond in the rough— the one who was worthy to enter the Cave of Wonders.

Late that night, Jafar disguised himself as an old prisoner in Aladdin's dungeon.

Jafar promised to set Aladdin free and reward him—in return for helping him find a special lamp.

Aladdin agreed. They slipped out of the dungeon and hurried off to the Cave of Wonders.

As Aladdin and Abu entered the cave, they heard a voice: "Touch nothing but the lamp." Soon, they found themselves in a huge cavern filled with coins and jewels. "Just a handful of this stuff would make me richer than the Sultan!" Aladdin exclaimed.

Suddenly, a beautifully woven carpet began floating around them. "A magic carpet!" cried Aladdin.

The carpet knew exactly what Aladdin and Abu were looking for and quickly led them into another chamber.

At the top of a high staircase, Aladdin saw the lamp. Just as he reached for it, Abu grabbed a large glittering ruby.

"Abu, no!" shouted Aladdin. But it was too late. The Cave of Wonders began to collapse around them!

With the Magic Carpet's help, Aladdin and Abu survived, but they found themselves trapped inside the dark cave.

"It looks like a beat-up, worthless piece of junk," said Aladdin as he rubbed the lamp. To his astonishment, the lamp began to glow, and in seconds, an enormous genie emerged!

The Genie grinned and said, "Wow! Does it feel good to be out of there! So what will it be, master?"

"You'll grant me any three wishes I want, right?" Aladdin said.
He didn't want to waste one of his wishes, so he tricked the Genie.
"Abu, he probably can't even get us out of this cave," Aladdin
teased. To prove his magical power, the Genie helped them escape.

"After I make my first two wishes, I'll use my third wish to set you free," Aladdin promised. But for his first wish, the young man asked, "Can you make me a prince?"

"One prince . . . coming up!" the Genie announced.

Meanwhile, Jafar had come up with a new evil plan. He would hypnotize the Sultan with his mystical snake staff. Then Jafar would marry Jasmine!

"You marry the princess—and then you become the Sultan!" Iago squawked.

That afternoon, Jafar began to cast a spell on the Sultan. But before he could finish, the doors of the throne room burst open and a handsome prince entered.

"I have journeyed from afar to seek your daughter's hand in marriage," announced Aladdin, disguised as Prince Ali.

"How dare you!" cried Jasmine, who had slipped in from the garden. "I am not a prize to be won."

Before Aladdin could respond, Jasmine ran from the room.

Aladdin, fearing he had lost Jasmine forever, asked the Genie for advice.

"Tell Jasmine the truth," the Genie suggested.

"No way!" said Aladdin. "But I will try to see her."

That night, he visited Jasmine in her room and took her for a ride on the Magic Carpet.

During the trip, Jasmine realized that Prince Ali was really the young man from the marketplace.

Later, Aladdin and Jasmine returned to the palace. They kissed good night, and at that moment, Aladdin realized she cared for him, too.

"For the first time in my life, things are finally starting to go right," Aladdin thought. But seconds later, the palace guards seized him.

On Jafar's orders, the guards tied Aladdin up, carried him to a high cliff, and tossed him into the sea.

Using his second wish, Aladdin was saved by the Genie.

Aladdin returned to the palace and revealed Jafar as a traitor. "Guards!" the Sultan commanded. "Arrest Jafar!"

But Jafar escaped. It was not too late, however, for the Sultan to see that Aladdin and Jasmine had fallen in love.

"You two will be wed," the Sultan said. Then he turned to Aladdin. "And you will become Sultan!"

Aladdin was worried. He didn't know how to be a sultan! He needed the Genie's help.

"Without you, I'm just Aladdin," he told the disappointed Genie. "I can't wish you free."

Later that day, Jafar had Iago steal the magic lamp. Jafar quickly summoned the Genie. "I wish to rule as Sultan," Jafar commanded. Sadly, the Genie had to obey.

For his second wish, Jafar asked to be a powerful sorcerer. He used his evil magic to make Jasmine and her father his slaves. Then Jafar banished Aladdin to the ends of the earth!

Fortunately, the Magic Carpet and Abu had been banished with him. Aladdin asked the Magic Carpet to take them back to Agrabah so that he could stop Jafar.

When Aladdin arrived in the palace, he realized he couldn't defeat Jafar, so he tricked him instead.

Aladdin convinced Jafar to use his third wish to become a genie. But Jafar had forgotten one very important thing—every genie must be imprisoned in a lamp! With Jafar gone, Aladdin happily made his third wish to free the Genie.

"No matter what anybody says, you'll always be a prince to me," the grateful Genie told Aladdin.

"That's right!" exclaimed the Sultan. "From this day forth, the princess shall marry whomever she wants!"

Of course Jasmine chose Aladdin. The young man's greatest wish had come true!